The Gift of the Magi

By O. Henry
Illustrated by Carol Heyer

Ideals Children's Books • Nashville, Tennessee

For my parents and mentors, William J. Heyer and
Merlyn M. Heyer...now and always.

—C.H.

Thanks to the models who posed for this book:

Suzan Davis Atkinson ....Della
David Atkinson ....Jim
Monique McAlonis ....Shopkeeper
Lee Riggan ....Hairdresser

Published by Ideals Children's Books
An imprint of Hambleton-Hill Publishing, Inc.
Nashville, Tennessee 37218

Printed and bound in Mexico

Library of Congress Cataloging-in-Publication Data
Henry, O., 1862–1910.
    The gift of the Magi / O. Henry ; illustrated by Carol Heyer.
       p.   cm.
    Summary: A simplified version of the well-known tale in which a
husband and wife sacrifice treasured possessions so that they may buy
each other Christmas presents.
    ISBN 1-57102-003-9
    [1. Christmas—Fiction. 2. Gifts—Fiction] I. Heyer, Carol, 1950– ill.
II. Title.
PZ7.H3964Gi   1994
[Fic]—dc20   94-4571
                                       CIP
                                        AC

The illustrations in this book were rendered in acrylics using live models.
The text type is set in Windsor.
The display type is set in Caslon Swash.
Color separations were made by Wisconsin Technicolor, Inc.
Printed and bound by R.R. Donnelley & Sons

10 9 8 7 6 5 4 3 2

ONE DOLLAR AND EIGHTY-SEVEN CENTS. THAT WAS ALL. AND SIXTY CENTS of it was in pennies. Pennies saved one and two at a time by bullying the grocer and the vegetable man and the butcher until her cheeks burned with embarrassment. Della counted it three times. Only one dollar and eighty-seven cents—and the next day would be Christmas.

There was clearly nothing to do but flop down on the faded little couch and cry. So Della did just that.

Her home was a furnished apartment that rented for $8 per week. It wasn't exactly shabby, but it had a feeling of hardship about it.

In the hallway below were a letter-box into which no letter would go and an electric buzzer that would not ring. On the letter-box was a card that read "Mr. James Dillingham Young." Its owner had called himself this grand name when his job had paid $30 per week. Now, when his income was only $20 per week, the card seemed a bit sad and ragged.

But when Mr. James Dillingham Young came home each night, he was called "Jim" and greatly hugged by Mrs. James Dillingham Young, already introduced to you as Della.

Della finished her crying and patted her cheeks with powder. She stood by the window and looked out dully at a gray cat walking on a gray fence in a gray backyard. Tomorrow would be Christmas Day, and she had only $1.87 to spend on a present for Jim. She had been saving every penny she could for months, but twenty dollars a week doesn't go far.

Expenses had been greater than she had thought they would be. They always are. Only $1.87 to buy a present for Jim. Her Jim. She had spent many happy hours planning to surprise him with something fine and rare—something worthy of the honor of being owned by Jim.

A tall mirror made from strips of glass hung on the wall between the windows of the room. Suddenly, Della whirled away from the window and stood before the mirror. Her eyes were shining brightly, but her face had lost its color. She quickly pulled down her hair and let it fall to its full length.

There were two possessions of the James Dillingham Youngs of which they were both very proud. One was Jim's gold watch that had belonged to his father and to his grandfather before that. The other was Della's hair.

Now Della's beautiful hair fell about her, down below her knees, rippling and shining like a cascade of brown waters. Then she put it up again nervously. She hesitated for a moment and stood still while a tear or two splashed on the worn red carpet.

Then she put on her old brown jacket and her old brown hat. With a whirl of skirts and with the sparkle still in her eyes, she fluttered out the door and down the stairs to the street.

Where she stopped the sign read: "Madame Sofronie, Hair Goods of All Kinds." Della ran up one flight of stairs and collected herself, panting. Madame was a large, pale woman with a chilly smile.

"Will you buy my hair?" asked Della.

"I buy hair," said Madame. "Take yer hat off and let's have a look at it."

The shining brown hair rippled down.

"I'll pay you twenty dollars for it," said Madame, lifting the heavy mass of hair with a practiced hand.

"Give it to me quick," said Della.

The next two hours flew by on rosy wings as Della went from store to store, searching for Jim's present.

She found it at last. It had surely been made for Jim and no one else. There was no other like it in any of the stores. It was a platinum watch chain, simple and pure in design. It was even worthy of The Watch. As soon as Della saw it, she knew that it must be Jim's. She paid twenty-one dollars for it and then hurried home with her remaining eighty-seven cents. With that chain on his watch, Jim could check the time in any company. As grand as the watch was, he was sometimes shy about looking at it because of the old leather strap he used instead of a chain.

When Della reached home her excitement fell away a little. She got out her curling irons and went to work repairing the damages made by her generosity—and by Madame Sofronie.

In forty minutes her head was covered with small, close-lying curls that made her look wonderfully like a mischievous schoolboy. She looked at her reflection in the mirror carefully.

"If Jim doesn't kill me first," she said to herself, "he'll say I look like a Coney Island chorus girl. But oh, what could I do with only a dollar and eighty-seven cents?"

At seven o'clock the coffee was made, and the frying pan was on the back of the stove, hot and ready to cook the chops.

Jim was never late. Della folded the watch chain in her hand and sat on the corner of the table near the door. When she heard his step on the stair, she panicked for just a moment. She had a habit of saying little silent prayers about the simple everyday things, and now she whispered, "Please God, make him think I am still pretty."

The door opened, and Jim stepped in. He looked thin and very serious. Poor fellow, he needed a new coat, and he had no gloves.

Jim stopped suddenly inside the door and stared at Della. There was an expression in his eyes that she could not read, and it terrified her. It was not anger, nor surprise, nor disapproval, nor horror, nor any of the things that she had expected. He simply stared at her with that strange expression on his face.

Della wriggled off the table and went to him.

"Jim, darling," she cried, "don't look at me that way. I had my hair cut off and sold it because I couldn't have lived through Christmas without giving you a present. You don't mind, do you? My hair grows awfully fast. Say 'Merry Christmas!' Jim, and let's be happy. You don't know what a nice, beautiful gift I've got for you."

Jim looked around the room curiously. "You say your hair is gone?" he said with disbelief.

"You needn't look for it," said Della. "It's sold and gone, I tell you. It's Christmas Eve, be good to me. Maybe the hairs of my head were numbered," she went on with a sudden serious sweetness, "but nobody could ever count my love for you. Shall I put the chops on, Jim?"

Jim seemed to wake from his trance, and he put his arms around Della. Then he took a package out of his coat pocket and threw it on the table.

"Don't make any mistake about me, Dell," he said, "I don't think there's anything in the way of a haircut or a shampoo that could make me love you any less. But if you'll unwrap that package, you'll see why I was so surprised at first."

Della's nimble fingers tore at the paper and string. She screamed with joy, but then her smiles quickly changed to tears.

For there lay The Combs—the set of hair combs that Della had admired for so long in a Broadway store window. They were beautiful combs, pure tortoise shell, with jeweled rims—just the color to wear in her beautiful vanished hair. They were expensive combs, she knew, and her heart had simply craved them without the slightest hope of ever owning them. And now, they were hers, but the hair that should have held them was gone.

She hugged them to her, and after a moment she was able to look up with a smile and say: "My hair grows so fast, Jim!"

And then Della leaped up and cried, "Oh, oh!"

Jim had not seen his beautiful present. She held it out to him eagerly. The dull precious metal seemed to flash with a reflection of her own bright spirit.

"Isn't it a dandy, Jim? I hunted all over town to find it. You'll have to look at your watch a hundred times a day now. Give me your watch. I want to see how it looks on it."

Instead of obeying, Jim tumbled down on the couch and put his hands under the back of his head and smiled.

"Dell," he said, "let's put our Christmas presents away and keep 'em a while. They're too nice to use just now. I sold the watch to get the money to buy your combs. And now suppose you put the chops on."

THE MAGI, AS YOU KNOW, WERE WISE MEN—WONDERFULLY WISE MEN— who brought gifts to the Babe in the manger. They invented the art of giving Christmas presents. Because they were wise, their gifts were wise. And here I have told you the story of two foolish children in a tiny apartment who unwisely gave up for each other the greatest treasures of their home.

But let it be said that of all those who give gifts, these two were the wisest. Of all who give gifts, those who give as these two did are the wisest. Everywhere they are the wisest. They are the Magi.

E   Henry, O.
Hen   The Gift of the Magi.